Mishmash

and the Sauerkraut Mystery

To
Ellen
a special friend of
Mishmash

Mishmash

and the Sauerkraut Mystery

MOLLY CONE

Illustrated by Leonard Shortall

HOUGHTON MIFFLIN COMPANY BOSTON

Also by MOLLY CONE

THE TROUBLE WITH TOBY
REENEY
THE REAL DREAM
ONLY JANE
TOO MANY GIRLS
MISHMASH
MISHMASH AND THE SUBSTITUTE TEACHER

1

Miss Patch was not at home. Importantly, Pete marched up the front walk. He rattled the doorknob, checked into the empty mailbox, and plucked a yellow handbill left on the top step. With a measuring eye, he looked out over Miss Patch's front lawn. The grass would need cutting tomorrow, he decided.

The door to the house next door opened and Mrs. Tribble who lived alone stuck her head out.

"The teacher's not home!" she shouted across the hedge to him. "She's gone to Europe!"

"I know!" Pete called back. "I'm taking care of her lawn while she's away."

Still eying him suspiciously, Mrs. Tribble pulled her head back in and closed her door.

Pete walked slowly around Miss Patch's house. Coming to the front again, he turned to face the living-room windows, and regarded them thought-fully. Something looked a little different than it had when he was here a few days ago. But he couldn't say exactly what.

He peered at the front of the house closely. The living-room window shade was pulled down tight. It hung a little crookedly. Pete swept his glance over the front yard, inspecting it with care. Then he went out the front gate and closed it securely behind him.

Wheeling his bike down the street, he passed the silent church and turned into the gas station on the corner.

"So the teacher's gone to Europe," the proprietor said as he watched Pete pump air into his bicycle tire.

"That's right!" said Pete.

"Took the dog with her, I suppose."

Pete shook his head. The thought of Mishmash going along with Miss Patch to Europe didn't seem at all strange to Pete. It was the sort of trip Mishmash would have enjoyed. Suddenly Pete felt a little sorry that Miss Patch hadn't thought of taking him herself.

"Not exactly," he said. "Miss Patch sent him to a very good dog kennel to board. He isn't the kind of dog you can go off and leave with just anyone, you know."

Pete wondered suddenly how Mishmash was getting along at the kennel. Mishmash wasn't the sort of dog who'd enjoy being locked up all the time with a bunch of dogs. He'd rather be with people. He didn't even like to sit outside in the middle of the road the way most dogs do. He liked sitting on chairs. Preferably one someone else wanted to sit on. Pete sighed, thinking that if his mother had allowed it, Mishmash could have stayed at his house while Miss Patch was in Europe.

The garage man grinned. "He used to walk right in. Just opened the door and walked right in. He's like no other dog I've ever met up with, that I'll say!" and the man laughed loudly as if he had said something funny.

Pete frowned.

Hastily the garage man said, "He's a friendly dog, all right. I don't mind telling you, I sort of miss him — in a manner of speaking — now and then."

"I sort of miss him myself," Pete said, and felt an odd lump in his throat. Quickly he turned to push his bike back to the street.

"He'll get along just fine at the kennels," the garage man shouted after him. "He'll have the time of his life!"

Pete rode up the block. He remembered how he had met Mishmash and Miss Patch on the same day. Only Miss Patch had been his new teacher, and Mishmash was supposed to have been his new dog. It was lucky for him, Pete decided, that his teacher had liked Mishmash better than his mother had.

Pete turned the corner and began to pedal up his own street. Halfway up, a truck was coming out of a driveway. Someone was moving into the new house on the block, Pete guessed. A small boy stood on the sidewalk in front of the house, waving his arms around, directing the truck driver.

"Hold it!" shouted the boy. "Now a little more to your left!"

Obediently, the truck veered to one side.

"Very good," the boy added in a grand manner. "Now let her go!"

The truck roared out of the driveway and up the street. Pete came to a stop in front of the new house. The little boy turned to stare curiously at Pete. His hair hung down in front almost to his eyes.

"Hi," the boy said. "You the Pete who lives around here?"

Pete nodded.

The newcomer grinned. "My name is Jules. Jules Ivar. I guess I'll be in your room at school."

Pete couldn't hide his surprise.

Jules smiled, turning one end of his mouth down while the other went up. It gave his face a mocking look.

"I was the shortest kid in my class," he stated through his twisted grin. "But I could run the fastest, hit the hardest, pitch the farthest, and if you want me to demonstrate, just say so."

Pete eyed the new boy with respect. He wished he could say he was the best, or the first, or the fastest at something. At the moment he couldn't think of anything he was extra good at.

He searched for something special to talk about. "Do you have a dog?"

"Used to," said Jules with a twisted expression. "But don't have him anymore. My mother doesn't like dogs."

"That's funny," said Pete. "That's exactly the way my mother felt about Mishmash!" He looked at Jules with real friendliness.

"Mishmash? I never heard of a dog with a name like that!"

"There isn't any other dog like Mishmash," Pete said. "He was my dog first. But my mother wouldn't let me keep him. I gave him to my teacher."

At Jules' look, Pete said, "You never saw a teacher like Miss Patch before either. She likes Mishmash just fine!"

"What's your favorite ice cream?" Jules asked suddenly.

Pete shrugged.

"Mine is pistachio. Some people have never even heard of pistachio," he said proudly.

"Is that so?" said Pete, pretending to be surprised.

"News report," muttered Jules, drawing the words out of the side of his mouth. "Girl coming."

Pete followed his glance.

"That's Wanda Sparling," Pete said, "Lives next door to me. In that yellow house."

Jules examined her thoughtfully. Wanda was staring at the cracks in the sidewalk as she walked, and every so often she weaved back and forth, hopping crazily.

"Not my dish," Jules commented, and turned away.

"She's not as dumb as she looks," Pete threw out, figuring he was being charitable at that.

"News report," muttered Jules. "No girl is as dumb as she looks!" And turning both ends of his mouth down at one time, he sat down comfortably on the curb.

"Jules!" a voice shouted from inside the house.

7

"I'd better go in," Jules said. "I have to unpack my collection." But he didn't move to get up.

They sat there together, watching Wanda move down the street toward them. She walked up to each house and rang the doorbell. Officiously she tapped a pencil on her wrist as she waited for the door to be answered. After each call, Wanda made careful notes in a notebook she carried in her pocket. She came toward them.

"Is your mother home, little boy?" she asked in a high prissy voice. She held her chin up in the air as she talked, and stared hard at Jules.

Hastily Pete said, "This is Jules Ivar. He's new here. He's in our grade at school. He was the fastest runner in his whole school where he came from!"

Wanda sniffed. "Well, you don't have to run that fast around here," she said in a high superior voice. "Nobody is going to be chasing after you." And Wanda, swishing her skirts from side to side, went up the path to his house. She rang the doorbell.

"How do you do, Mrs. Ivar," she said in a

showy voice when Jules' mother opened the door. "I'm Wanda Sparling. My mother is having a rummage sale Saturday in our backyard. And you're invited to come and have coffee and buy anything you like."

Mrs. Ivar regarded Wanda with astonishment. "A rummage sale?" she said blankly.

Wanda nodded briskly. "In our backyard. Everybody in the neighborhood is coming. You don't have to buy anything if you don't want to," she added generously. "My mother is serving coffee and cake anyway."

"Well, I don't know," Mrs. Ivar said carefully. She looked over Wanda's head and caught sight of the two boys. "Jules!" she called sharply. "If you don't get in here and take care of this collection of old hats you left here, I declare I'm going to give it to this little girl for her mother's rummage sale!"

With a cry of rage, Jules hurtled up the walk. He brushed passed Wanda and stamped into the house. The door closed behind him and his mother too.

Wanda shrugged, and came down the walk toward Pete.

Wrathfully, Pete said, "Don't you know it's not polite to go around asking people for things before they even move in!"

Wanda stuck her chin up in the air and put away her notebook. "I wasn't asking for anything." A curious light came into her eyes. "That Jules, he collects *hats!*"

"That's so," said Pete with admiration. He gazed at the closed door. He wished he had thought of collecting hats. He let his mouth twist a little as Jules' did.

"You'd better be careful or your face might just get stuck that way," Wanda warned. "You even look a little bit like him already." Her tone was uncomplimentary.

"Funny you should say that," Pete said thoughtfully. "My face being like Jules Ivar's, I mean. Because it so happens that in some things we're just exactly alike. In some things," he said softly.

Wanda snorted. "Like what things?"

"Pistachio," he said lovingly. And was pleased

to see the bewildered look on Wanda's face. He turned his face up to the sun, sucked in his lips, turned his mouth down, and half closed his eyes.

"What's the matter?" Wanda asked. "You got a stomach-ache?"

"Even our interests are alike," Pete went on. "Of course, his being the fastest runner and all that — " Pete shrugged. "My time will come," he said philosophically.

"You bet it will," said Wanda. "And not soon enough if you ask me!"

Pete began to feel a little sorry for Wanda. He gave her one of Jules' smiles as she moved on down the block.

Happily Pete pushed his bike toward home. He stopped once and pulled at his hair so it hung down over his forehead. His hair wasn't really long enough, he thought regretfully.

Pete put his bike into the garage.

His mother looked up as he entered the kitchen. Her eyes rested on him for a moment. "Perhaps you'd better run down and get a haircut," she said absently.

"A haircut!" Pete raised his voice in an exclamation of despair. It reminded him of Jules Ivar. His mother jumped a little.

"I don't really need a haircut," he said softly, and started up the stairs.

Mrs. Peters stood where she was a few moments, looking after him, and as he reached the door to his room, he heard her sigh.

Pete tried out his new expression before his mirror. He did look quite a bit like Jules Ivar, he thought, practicing Jules Ivar's squint. Looking into the mirror, he rested his face a moment.

Suddenly, unaccountably, he remembered the living-room window shade of Miss Patch's house being down. It seemed to him, now he thought about it, that Miss Patch had left it halfway up. An odd prickle began at the back of his neck. He rolled his head around on his shoulders.

"Guess I must have been mistaken!" he said loudly. Then he looked with round clear eyes into the mirror and knew that he had not been mistaken at all.

2

"A NEW FAMILY moved into the neighborhood yesterday," Pete's mother said at breakfast the next morning.

"That so?" said Mr. Peters. But he wasn't much interested. He rattled the newspaper as he turned it.

"A little boy, I think," Mrs. Peters said.

"News report," said Pete with Jules' smile. "He only looks little. He's the same age I am."

"Oh?" said his mother with real interest.

"His name is Jules. Jules Ivar. He collects hats."

Mr. Peters looked up from his newspaper. "Hats?"

"News report," said Pete. "Those things you wear above your ears." He turned his mouth down at both corners.

His mother and father exchanged glances.

"Y'know it's funny," Pete said, squinting the way Jules did when he talked, as if he were saying something very important. He was pleased to see that he had his parents' complete attention. Mr. Peters even set down his newspaper, his eyes fastened on Pete's face.

"About collecting hats, I mean. It's kind of funny to think Jules Ivar has a whole collection of hats when it's just exactly what I've been thinking of doing for some time now."

His mother looked surprised. "Hats?" she said.

"Interesting," his father said in that dry voice he used when he wasn't at all interested. He went back to his newspaper.

Pete turned his full attention on his mother. "It's sort of an unusual hobby, if you know what I mean."

Mr. Peters opened out his paper. "I bet I could name you a half-dozen women living on this block who have collected a closetful of hats this season already!"

Mrs. Peters smiled.

"I wasn't talking about ladies' hats!" Pete said.

His father only grunted. Something in the newspaper had caught his eye. He said suddenly to Pete, "Do you have a padlock and chain for your bicycle?"

Pete shrugged. "I guess so."

"Well, you'd better start using it. There seems to be a rash of bicycle thefts this month."

His father's voice was matter-of-fact. Almost as if he were talking about an outbreak of the measles. But Mrs. Peters suddenly began to look worried.

"You mean right in this neighborhood?" she said.

But Mr. Peters had already turned the page. "Here's an odd one," he said with a grin. "Some hoodlum made off with six cases of sauerkraut. Police are on the lookout for the sauerkraut thief, it says." He chuckled. "They figure the burglar must be from out of town. Our local police have no record of sauerkraut lovers living around here."

Pete moved uneasily. "You mean he's hiding out somewhere around here?"

"Could be," said Mr. Peters as if it didn't matter

much. "But I wouldn't worry about it if I were you. Your mother doesn't hoard sauerkraut. As long as she sticks to diamonds, we're okay," he said grandly.

Mrs. Peters gave him only a small smile.

Pete gazed at his empty bowl. Then he shook more Cheerios into it, sprinkled sugar over the cereal, steeped it in milk, and sat there looking at it. He thought of the shade pulled down tight at Miss Patch's house when she had left it halfway up.

"As soon as you finish cutting the lawn over at Miss Patch's house, you can run over the lawn right here," Mr. Peters said generously.

"Maybe I should do our lawn at home here first," Pete said, with sudden eagerness.

His mother looked at him reflectively. But his father didn't seem to notice.

"No need of that," Mr. Peters said. "You might as well hop right out after breakfast and get your work done over there."

A little later, Pete was moving slowly down the sidewalk.

"Step on a crack, break your mother's back!"

Wanda shouted after him. Though Pete pretended not to hear, he found himself moving more hesitantly, not putting his feet directly on the cracks in the sidewalk squares.

Jules Ivar was practicing pitching a baseball against his garage door. On his head was a hat. A hat with a high round crown and a stiff narrow brim sticking out all around. Pete stopped to stare at it.

"It's my English bobby's hat," Jules said without interrupting his pitching. "That's what they call policemen in England. Bobbies."

Pete eyed the hat respectfully.

"Pretty good!" he called out when Jules hit the chalked-in bull's-eye with his baseball.

"News report," Jules said out of the side of his mouth. "That's better than good!"

Pete nodded with admiration.

Jules trotted over to the front walk. "I practice all the time," he said breathlessly. "Every chance I get. I'm going to be the best pitcher in your school!"

Pete looked at him reflectively. "John Williams

18

was the best last year. He's pretty big."

Jules smiled as if Pete had said just what he had been waiting for. "That's to my advantage then. I can always beat them if they're big. That's because I'm fast!"

He tossed Pete a ball. "Throw me a few just for practice."

Pete threw the ball from one hand to the other. "I'd like to, but I can't. I have a summer job. Taking care of the teacher's lawn. She's not home. She won't be home practically all summer."

Jules gave Pete a strange look. "You mean no one is living in her house right now? It's empty?"

"That's the way she left it," Pete said, and thought, uncomfortably, of the window shade being down.

Jules didn't seem to notice the careful answer.

"Here," Pete said, and returned the ball.

"I used to collect balls." Jules turned his mouth upside down again. "With players' autographs and that kind of thing." He shrugged. "I like having a ball in my hand, when I'm not doing anything else, I mean. Keeps me in practice."

Jules turned back to his garage door bull's-eye. Pressing his mouth into an upside-down crease, he wound up and pitched the ball. It smacked directly onto the center of the garage door. Jules didn't even grunt. He went right on pitching.

Pete continued on down the street. He wished he had remembered to bring his ball. It was funny now that he thought about it, how much alike he and Jules really were. Carrying a ball around, for instance. That's the way he felt too. Sort of comfortable with a ball in his hand. Suddenly he wished he had brought his baseball along with him.

He picked up a rock from the gutter and tossed it up and down as he walked. Then as he cut across the empty lot on the other side of the church, he found an old tennis ball. It wasn't much. But it was better than nothing. He tossed it high into the air and caught it — expertly.

Pete whistled loudly as he pulled the lawn mower out from under the porch of Miss Patch's house. The shade was still down tight. He ran the mower speedily up and down the lawn, not being too careful at the corners. It was only that he was anxious to get back and toss a ball around with Jules Ivar, he told himself, and looked quickly over his shoulder at the house.

He finished cutting the front lawn and went around to the back. The kitchen window looked out onto the backyard. Hurriedly Pete ran the mower up and down the grass there. Making two quick runs, he stopped for breath. A dull clunk, as if someone had dropped something, reached his ears. Quickly he glanced up at the kitchen window. He listened carefully. Then he grinned a little shamefacedly and pushed the lawn mower up and down a few more times. When he reached the end of the row, he glanced up again at the window. He listened . . .

He heard only the far-off sound of a TV. It was coming from the little old house next door.

Pete put away the lawn mower. He stood in the middle of the front yard a moment facing the shade-covered window. The house was empty. Anyone could clearly see that.

The window shade was down tight. The front

door was shut and locked. The welcome mat was rolled up. An empty milk bottle lay on its side in the corner of the front porch. Pete looked at the milk bottle. He hadn't noticed a milk bottle there before.

Pete's hands shook a little as he took out his ball. He tossed it up and down in the air and tried to shake off the sudden odd feeling that came over him. As if something or somebody from inside that empty house was watching him.

He threw his ball up but missed it as it came down because he had cast a quick look out of the corner of his eyes at the window. Scrambling to collect the ball under the shrubbery, he felt his face turn hot — just as if he knew someone had been watching him.

Pete dropped back into the cover of the shrubbery. An empty house with a hedge all the way around, with only an old church on one side, and a little old lady living in the house on the other side would be an ideal hideout. Pete thought of the report in the morning paper. The sauerkraut thief. He held his breath and peered out at the house. His heart began to pound loudly. He could hear its thumps in his chest. Then he heard Mrs. Tribble come out on the porch next door and call to her cat and go back in again.

Feeling a little foolish, he got up and moved purposefully toward the porch. He climbed the steps, took the broom from off the hook behind the post and briskly swept. He put the broom back again.

Whistling loudly, he put out his hand to rattle the doorknob — and the whistle died in his throat. Under his hand, the knob turned easily. The door slowly opened.

Pete jumped. He jumped so far back that he fell off the porch. Then he got up and ran. But not very far. For something flew out after him. It tangled up his legs and threw him down.

Something big and black with a long wet tongue and joyful hoarse barks.

"MISHMASH!" shouted Pete.

It wasn't a thief at all. It was Mishmash!

Mishmash sat back on his hind legs. His eyes gleamed happily. His mouth opened and his teeth stuck out in a friendly grin. It reminded Pete of Miss Patch. It reminded him that Mishmash was Miss Patch's dog and she was in Europe. Pete frowned.

"You're not supposed to be here, Mishmash!" he scolded. "You're supposed to be staying at the dog kennel until Miss Patch gets back."

Mishmash only blinked.

Pete thought of the dog kennel. It was wired all around like a chicken coop. There weren't any plants to dig up, or old shoes to bury. Pete found it hard to blame Mishmash for leaving.

"You have to go back, Mishmash!" Pete said.

Mishmash backed away. With one eye on Pete, he stepped carefully up the porch steps, walked through the open front door and pushed it shut quickly behind him.

3

"I've never heard of a dog living alone," said Wanda suspiciously.

"It isn't as if it were for permanent," Pete explained patiently. "He probably stuck it out at the dog kennel as long as he could stand it. You can't blame him for wanting to come home. Looks to me as if he's just sort of housekeeping for himself until Miss Patch gets back."

"A dog housekeeping!" cried Wanda.

Pete looked quickly around. They were sitting in Wanda's garage amidst a pile of boxes which had been set out there for the rummage sale.

"Well, there's nothing in the law that says a dog can't set up housekeeping if he wants to," Pete said in a loud whisper.

"That's because there's never been a dog who

even thought of setting up housekeeping," said Wanda.

"Well, there's no law against it," Pete said.

"I guess they've just never caught a dog yet who's tried living alone. But I bet if the police catch him . . ."

Pete glared at her. "They're not going to! Y'hear me!"

Wanda glared back. "They certainly will if he's going to be silly enough to expect the milkman to give him delivery service. My mother says milkmen tell everything they see." Wanda put her hand up to her mouth to smother a giggle. "Only not to her, she says. She says she's always the last one on the block to know."

Pete kicked at a corner of a box of junk. "Personally, I think he'll get along just fine. After all, all he has to do is lie low."

"You're lucky," said Wanda. "So long as the police are busy looking for that sauerkraut thief, they won't pay much attention to a dog."

Pete frowned. He had completely forgotten about the sauerkraut thief. Suddenly he remembered how Mishmash had once taken the welcome mat from the neighbor's front porch, and how he had made off with the bottom half of a pair of pajamas hanging on the line, and how he had snitched an old fur neckpiece off a railing.

"Of course, he's pretty smart — for a dog," Wanda admitted, following her own thoughts. "He's the only dog my mother's ever heard of who opens the door and remembers to close it behind him." Wanda grinned. "My mother says that's smarter than some kids!"

Pete thought of Mishmash — and the missing sauerkraut cans. He wondered how Mishmash had managed to do it. He glanced quickly at Wanda, and then away again. He wasn't exactly sure about Wanda. If she suspected that Mishmash was the sauerkraut thief, she might think she had to report it to the police. Pete pretended to be interested in looking at the contents of the box of junk.

Wanda went right on talking.

"If I were a thief, you know what I would do? I'd find a nice empty house — where someone's gone on a vacation or something, and just hide out with the stuff until the coast was clear. That's what I'd do!" She raised her eyebrows significantly.

Pete snorted. "Mishmash doesn't have to worry about going anywhere — " He stopped suddenly, curled up his tongue and pretended he was looking for something in the box.

"I wasn't talking about Mishmash," Wanda said with new meaning.

Pete held up the old clock he had pulled out of the box of junk. He shook it and wound it up. It ticked loudly, but the hands didn't move. It wasn't much good, he decided and tossed it back into the box. Wanda was still regarding him curiously.

"You don't think he'll try running the washing machine or anything?" Pete pretended to be worried, but he wasn't really thinking about it.

"Nothing Mishmash did would surprise *me!*" Wanda said with a sniff, and looked someplace else. "Sometimes I think he doesn't even know he's a dog."

Pete remembered something. "Anyway, Miss Patch doesn't have a washing machine. She takes her stuff to the laundromat next to the super-market."

Wanda sat up straight. "When?"

Pete thought about it. "At night I guess. Or maybe Sunday mornings."

"Well, that's all right then," Wanda said in re-lief. "Hardly anybody ever bothers going into the laundromat once dinner is over, my uncle says. He owns that one."

Pete remembered Mishmash locking him out of Miss Patch's house. "He isn't one you can reason with," he said.

Wanda bristled. "He is too. My uncle is a very reasonable man. He says so himself. All the time."

Pete turned his mouth down into his new grimace. "I don't mean your uncle," he said softly. "I mean Mishmash."

"Oh him! You won't catch me reasoning with a dog."

"Personally, I'd rather reason with Mishmash than with some people I know."

Wanda eyed him with suspicion.

Pete moved among the boxes of junk. He picked

up a sailor hat and stuck it on his head. He wondered if Jules Ivar had a sailor hat in his collection.

"Keep your hands off the merchandise!" Wanda warned. "Nothing's for sale until Saturday. D'you hear me?"

"The whole neighborhood can hear you," Pete said. "Anyway who would want a little old hat like that?"

"Lots of people will want lots of these things," Wanda said. "People always want what other people have. My father says that's the key to our economic system."

"Personally I wouldn't want any of this stuff," said Pete, screwing up his face.

Wanda regarded him. "Not even an English bobby's hat? The kind that Jules Ivar was wearing this morning?"

Pete thought of the hat with its high round crown and its turned-out brim. "You've got one?" he asked carefully.

"Oh, you wouldn't want it," said Wanda airily. "It's just some of that useless stuff my mother collected for the rummage sale."

"Let me see it!" said Pete, not even trying to hide his eagerness. He could just see himself. Strolling down the street, tossing his baseball into the air, wearing this little old hat. "Oh, it's been lying around for ages," he'd say offhandedly.

"I'll take it right now!" he said to Wanda.

"You will not!" said Wanda. "Nothing is for sale yet. Not until Saturday. Besides, I might want to keep it for my costume collection."

"Costume collection!" Pete hooted. "Since when have you got a costume collection?"

Wanda eyed him carefully. "Oh, just about as long as you've had your hat collection."

Pete creased his face into Jules Ivar's very deepest grimace, and walked away. He went down to Jules Ivar's house.

He sat on the front steps and whistled, but Jules didn't stick his head out the door. Then he went around to the backyard. Mrs. Ivar was hanging some sleeping bags on the clothes line.

"Oh, it's you," she said, and smiled.

"Is Jules home?" Pete asked politely.

33

"He's running," said Mrs. Ivar. She flapped at the line.

Pete looked at her blankly.

"His quarter of a mile," she said. "Every day he runs a quarter of a mile. He's not very big," she added automatically, "but he's pretty fast."

"I'll tell him you stopped by to play," she called after Pete.

Pete continued up the block, walking a short distance. Then he began to jog, lifting his knees high and bending his elbows. He had often run this way up and down the block, he recalled now, and it struck him as not at all strange that there was Jules out somewhere doing the same thing. Pete increased his speed a little. Reaching his own house, he ran around and around it and finally flopped down on the back steps.

Mrs. Peters opened the door. "For goodness sakes," she said. "It's much too warm to be dashing around like that — besides it's dinnertime."

Breathing deeply, Pete went upstairs to wash his hands.

Sitting at the dinner table, he thought of Mishmash having the nerve to walk right out of that place where they boarded dogs. He thought of him coming straight home to Miss Patch's house where he belonged. Pete grinned. "Good old Mishmash," he almost said aloud. Then he looked quickly up at his parents, and down at his plate.

"The news report on the radio said they haven't found the sauerkraut thief yet," Mrs. Peters said with a worried air.

"A matter of time," Mr. Peters said comfortably, and served Pete a helping of roast beef.

Pete pressed his mouth down into Jules Ivar's favorite expression. He guessed he'd better warn Mishmash to lay off the pilfering.

His father looked at him and frowned, and his mother said quickly, "Wanda tells me you'll be helping her with her rummage sale."

"I will not!" Pete said.

"Rummage sale?" said Mr. Peters.

"In Mrs. Sparling's backyard," said Mrs. Peters. "She is taking everything out of her attic and inviting the neighbors to come over." She looked thoughtfully out the window. "I wonder if she happens to have an old umbrella stand."

Mr. Peters stopped eating. "You mean that woman intends to sell all her old junk to her neighbors!"

Mrs. Peters smiled. "Mrs. Sparling has some lovely things put away in her attic. Things she just grew tired of. I wonder if she's planning to get rid of that old cut-glass bowl she used to have."

Mr. Peters was looking at her with a bewildered expression. Pete grinned.

"Wanda is expecting you to help her right after dinner," Mrs. Peters said to Pete.

With a twist Pete turned his grin into a grimace. Then he finished his dinner quickly and went out. But he didn't go over to Wanda's. He went down the street to Jules Ivar's house. A pile of stuff was sitting in the driveway. A sleeping bag was the first thing Pete noticed. Then a baseball bat, a laundry bag and a length of rope. He looked at the gear curiously.

"You going somewhere?" Pete asked as Jules came out of the garage carrying a duffel bag.

"To camp," Jules said, and his voice rose so

loud that his mother's face appeared at the window. She smiled and nodded, pointing to the watch on her arm.

"I'm supposed to catch the bus," Jules said. He looked thoughtfully down the street.

Pete stood around and watched Jules tie a couple of items together. He wished he had gone to camp this summer. If he had gone to camp he wouldn't have been home to take care of Miss Patch's lawn. Pete thought of Mishmash housekeeping for himself and he sighed.

"Every year I go to this camp," Jules explained. "I've won every medal they've got" — he paused to twist his face into a kind of grin — "except the swimming medal."

Pete looked at him admiringly. "I guess this time you'll get that," Pete said.

"I guess so," Jules said offhandedly. He stood a moment without speaking, staring at his stuff.

"I'll write to you," Pete said eagerly.

Jules jerked his head up. "You'd better not! Last year I didn't get any of the mail until after I got home. It's because the camp is off the regular route or something. My mother says she isn't even going to bother to write me any letters. I'm going to have to keep her informed, she said." It sounded as if Jules was more pleased than not at this.

Pete looked at him closely.

"How's the job?" Jules said as if he were really interested.

For a moment Pete thought he would tell Jules all about Mishmash housekeeping for himself. Then he decided he had better not. He had already told Wanda, and there were times he wished he hadn't.

"All right, I guess," Pete said, looking away.

"What do you do there?" Jules asked. "I mean do you have to go inside or anything?"

Pete shook his head. "Keep the lawn cut, and the papers picked up. It isn't much," he said as if it wasn't very much.

"Too bad I'm leaving for camp. Else I could keep you company."

"Too bad," Pete repeated.

"You go over there every day?" Jules asked.

Pete shrugged. "Not every day exactly. Just when things need tending to. Not tomorrow anyway." What he was going to do tomorrow, he just decided, was to go to the supermarket and buy some dog food. Not the supermarket in his neighborhood, but the one way over the other side of town. "I have to cut our own lawn tomorrow," he added. But he made a face at the thought.

Jules reached into his back pocket and pulled out a neatly rolled hat. It was his English bobby's hat. He certainly liked that English bobby's hat, thought Pete as he watched Jules place it carefully on his head. Pete looked at it closely. It was exactly like the one he had seen in Wanda's garage. Exactly.

Jules raised one hand in farewell and twisted his face into a grin. "Tally ho!" he said.

"Tally ho!" said Pete, and went back up the street. What he had to do, he decided, was figure out a way to get his hands on the other hat. He thought of Wanda keeping it for herself and the twist that came to his lips could very well have been Jules' own.

4

HOLDING THE PACKAGE of dog food under his arm, Pete knocked lightly at Miss Patch's front door.

"Mishmash?" he called softly.

There was a snuffling sound as if Mishmash was listening on the other side of the door.

"It's me, Pete!" Pete said.

There was a soft patter, then silence.

Pete rattled the doorknob a little impatiently. "Mishmash!" he said, and glanced quickly over his shoulder.

An old man was leaning over the gate peering at him. "There's no one home there, boy," he called to Pete. "It's locked up tight. Nobody home."

"Oh!" said Pete, as if it were new to him. He

smiled weakly. "Well, thanks," he said, and waited until the man had walked down the block and turned the corner.

Leaving the dog food there on the porch behind the post, Pete sneaked around to the backyard. The back door was locked too, and a pillow was laid out to air over the porch railing. Pete pulled it off.

"Mishmash!" he called out, and rattled the back doorknob.

The shade snapped up on the kitchen door window. Through the glass, Mishmash grinned at him. Behind him Pete could see a pile of blankets on the floor. On the kitchen table stood a box of Cheerios and a bowl. Pete guessed it was lucky he had thought of bringing the dog food or else Mishmash would be eating all Miss Patch's supplies.

Pete pointed to the pillow under his arm, shook his head, and frowned meaningfully.

The doorbell rang at the front door, and Mishmash, looking suddenly happy, dropped out of sight. Pete ran down the steps, and then back up again to stuff the pillow into the box Miss Patch always left on the porch to hold milk bottles. Then he galloped around the house to the front door.

A man was just going back down the walk. He carried a briefcase in one hand and a brush in the other.

"Is the lady of the house at home?" he turned to ask politely.

Pete mounted the steps and stood with his back to the door. Pete thought of the pillow set out to air. He hoped Mishmash wouldn't think *he* was the lady of the house. Pete put his hand on the doorknob behind him, holding the door closed, just in case.

"Nobody is home here," he said loudly. "I'm the boy who cuts the lawn."

The man smiled. "Well, I left my catalogue. My telephone number is written on the backside," he said.

Pete called after him. "She's gone to Europe!" But he had already shut the gate.

Pete picked up the catalogue and stuck it into his pocket. He'd better take that away with him, he decided, before Mishmash decided he had to have a new broom or something. He looked at the closed door. It remained tightly shut.

He waited awhile, sitting there on the top step, hoping Mishmash would decide to unlock the door and listen to him. Finally Pete took the lawn mower out from under the porch and began to cut the lawn. It didn't need cutting, but he had to have some excuse for sticking around so long, so he cut it again.

As he was putting the lawn mower away again, Mrs. Tribble came out of the house next door. She stood on the porch and beckoned to him.

Uneasily he went over.

"You the boy who was cutting the lawn here day before yesterday?" she said. She came down the porch steps to peer into his face.

He nodded, wondering.

"Well, I can't see so good since I got my new glasses," she exclaimed, "and I just thought I'd better make sure." She looked at him a little worriedly. "Last night I thought I heard some funny noises," she said. "From over there," and she jerked her head in the direction of Miss Patch's house.

Pete tried to look surprised.

"Noises?"

"Tappings," she said, "and rappings, and that sort of thing." She pulled her shawl a little closer about her shoulders and leaned close to him. "Poltergeists!" she said.

"What?" said Pete.

She nodded wisely. "I remember my old grandma telling me when I was a little girl. They get into empty houses sometimes."

"What do they look like?" asked Pete uneasily.

She looked up toward the shade that was drawn down on her side of the house. "You can't see them," she whispered. "But you can always hear them. They're ghosts! That's what they are!"

Pete tried not to smile. Probably what she had heard was Mishmash.

"Nobody's ever been able to do anything about getting rid of poltergeists," she said.

Out of the corner of his eye, Pete could see the door to Miss Patch's house opening slowly. He said quickly, "Well, if you can't really see them, I guess you don't have to worry about them."

She frowned thoughtfully. "One of them makes noises like an old vacuum cleaner."

Pete wondered suddenly whether Mishmash was cleaning house. He thought of the pillow set out to air. He looked worriedly around behind him. The door was closed again, and the package of dog food was gone.

"Well, I don't like it!" said Mrs. Tribble sharply. "I can tell you I don't like it. People who own houses should live in them. There should be a law!" She turned to go back into her house.

Pete returned to Miss Patch's yard. He sat down on the front step. He couldn't help smiling.

A lady wheeling a buggy came slowly down the street. When she saw Pete, she stopped and nodded.

"Hello there," she called. "When did the teacher get back from Europe?"

Pete got up and went down to the gate. "She's not exactly home yet," he said, and looked at the baby in the buggy. "She won't be home for at least a couple of weeks yet."

The woman looked surprised. "That's funny!"

she said. "I thought I saw lights on last night." She gazed curiously over Pete's head up to the house.

Pete swallowed. "Sometimes it looks just as if lights are on in the house. Some houses are funny that way."

She gave a little laugh. "Well, maybe you're right," she said. "My husband says I'm always imagining things." She smiled and went on.

Pete went out the gate and looked after her.

He guessed he had nothing really to worry about. He grimaced, making it as much like Jules Ivar's as possible. He enjoyed the way his mouth stretched, and liked the feeling of the hard place it left on his chin. Pete moved along toward home whistling happily.

Wanda was waiting for him, sitting on his front porch. He took his baseball out of his pocket and threw it up and down as he walked along. He even frowned a couple of times like Jules Ivar. But Wanda looked as if she was pretending not to notice.

"News report," Pete muttered out of the side of his mouth. He told her about Mrs. Tribble's poltergeists and the lady who was always imagining things. "Everything's going like a house on fire!" he said with satisfaction.

Wanda looked at him doubtfully. "I never heard of a dog turning lights on and off."

"There never was a dog like Mishmash," Pete said proudly.

"I've been thinking," Wanda said, sitting on the porch with her chin in her hands. "Could be it's not Mishmash there alone at all. Could be" — her voice suddenly sounded hollow — "the sauerkraut thief!"

Pete pressed his lips together and smiled widely. If Wanda hadn't guessed that Mishmash himself was probably the sauerkraut thief, he wasn't going to be the one to tell her.

5

PETE'S SATISFACTION lasted right through dinner. He even figured he'd offer to help Wanda a bit with her rummage sale. But when she came out of her house, she looked at him with a sour expression.

"My uncle's here. The one who owns the laundromat."

Pete took his hands out of his pockets. He thought of the vacuum cleaner noises Mrs. Tribble had heard, and the pillow airing on the railing. He thought of the pile of blankets, like new wash, on the kitchen floor. And he slowly sat down on the porch steps.

"You mean he's taken the washing into the laundromat!" His voice came in a hoarse whisper.

"And everybody else's out!" Wanda said. "He sneaked in early this morning between customers and dumped all the clean wet wash onto the dirty floor, and stuck his old blankets inside. Is my uncle mad! He says if that customer ever comes around again, he's going to have her arrested."

Pete looked up in surprise. "You mean he doesn't know who it was!"

Wanda giggled. "Someone told him whoever it is owns a big black dog. They thought they saw the dog waiting inside. My uncle is out there making a big sign to put on the door. It says NO DOGS ALLOWED. He thinks that's going to fix things," she said.

"It won't fix anything," Pete reminded her. "Mishmash can't read."

Wanda gave him a pitying glance. "It's not for the dog; it's for the lady who owns the dog."

Pete sighed. "That's all right then!"

Wanda grimaced. "Just wait until they find out there is no lady," she said.

Pete stretched out his legs. "Probably Mishmash won't even go near the place again. He's probably just about finished with the housecleaning anyway." Pete smiled.

"Then you'd better start worrying!" Wanda said.

Pete raised his eyebrows the way Jules Ivar did when he looked at you without asking a question.

"When Mishmash is through with the house-cleaning — *if* it's Mishmash who's doing the house-cleaning," she added darkly — "what's he going to do next!"

Pete scratched his head.

At breakfast the next morning, Mrs. Peters said, "The milkman told me he saw something funny at Miss Patch's house yesterday."

"What did he mean by 'funny'?" Pete asked, but he had a feeling he already knew.

"He said that when he went to check on the milk box he found a pillow stuffed inside."

"Is that so!" said Pete pretending he had never heard of such a thing.

"I wonder why she would leave a pillow inside of her milk box," Mr. Peters said, gazing thoughtfully at the ceiling.

Pete gave his very best imitation of Jules Ivar's

grimace, but all it did was to make the wrinkles on his mother's forehead deepen.

"Have you a pain somewhere?" she asked.

Pete looked at her, feeling a little surprised. "Who, me?"

His father's glance settled on him. "Is there anybody else sitting in your chair right at this moment?" Mr. Peters asked politely.

"What makes you say that?" Pete said.

"I thought perhaps I was the one who was mistaken," Mr. Peters said, and drank his cup of coffee.

"Mrs. Sparling is having her rummage sale today," Mrs. Peters said quickly.

And for some reason no one said anything more through the rest of the breakfast.

Pete was just passing through the hallway when the telephone rang.

"I've got it!" he shouted and picked up the receiver. "Pete Peters speaking," he said.

"The boy who cuts the lawn?" The voice had a crackled sound. It was Mrs. Tribble.

Pete gulped. "Yes," he said, and waited.

"There's a pack of dogs playing games in Miss Patch's backyard . . ."

"Games!" shouted Pete into the telephone.

"That's right! Just a minute."

Pete held the receiver tightly to his ear. He heard a humming sound and his nose began to twitch as if a dusty curtain had been whisked aside.

"Yup. They're playing games all right. They're all in a circle and one of them is running around and around. There!" she hollered. "He dropped it!"

"Dropped what?" Pete said.

"I dunno. I can't make it out." The voice drifted off, as if the woman had turned her head. "I can't see too well," she said. "But it appears to me — yes, by jiminy, that's what it is. A bone." The woman made clicking noises under her tongue.

"Young man!" she shouted into the telephone. "If it's your job to take care of things for Miss Patch, you'd better get yourself over here before those wild animals tear up the rosebushes!" She slammed down the receiver.

Hastily Pete set the telephone back on the table.

He ran next door. Wanda was sitting out in her backyard painting signs. ODDS AND ENDS she had lettered. ANYTHING for 25¢. Mrs. Sparling was going back and forth carrying dishes out to a table set under the apple tree.

"Pssst!" said Pete.

Wanda carefully painted in two exclamation points. She raised her head inquiringly.

"Mishmash is giving a party," Pete said hoarsely.

Wanda knocked over her box of colors. "What!" she shrieked.

Pete glanced at Wanda's mother across the yard. But she was too busy to notice them.

"He's got all the dogs in the neighborhood over in Miss Patch's backyard and it sounds as if they might be playing drop the handkerchief. Except they're not using a handkerchief, they're using an old bone."

"I guess the house is all cleaned up then, if he's giving a party." Wanda giggled. "I wonder if he's planning on serving refreshments."

"I never thought about his giving a party," Pete said.

"Next thing you know he'll be taking in boarders. That is," she added with a meaningful glance, "if he hasn't already."

Pete regarded Wanda reflectively. She still hadn't guessed that the sauerkraut thief was probably Mishmash himself.

"That's what my aunt does," Wanda said. "She doesn't like living alone so she rents her front room to tourists. It keeps things humming, she says." Wanda blinked her eyes. "Of course my aunt's not a dog."

Pete looked out over the apple trees. Miss Patch's house was just around the corner from the street that ran into the highway. He didn't really believe that Mishmash . . .

Wanda's mother came out on the porch with a stack of cups in her hands. "Wanda!" she called.

Wanda stood up. "Don't go letting on to Mishmash about our rummage sale," she warned. "My mother is expecting the principal's wife and the garden club president and a lot of other important ladies." Wanda raised her chin haughtily. "It's a fancy party. We're restricting it to people."

Pete glared after her. Then he turned and trotted down the street toward Miss Patch's.

Mishmash's guests had already gone home when Pete got there, and the dog was sitting comfortably under the hydrangea bush. On his face was an expression that reminded Pete of his mother after she had entertained successfully at an afternoon of bridge.

"Now look here, Mish," Pete said, dropping down beside him. "You have to lay off the parties, you understand? No more having company or you'll find yourself in trouble."

Mishmash raised his eyebrows.

"Real trouble!" said Pete.

Mish yawned.

Pete lay back under the bush with his head on Mish's flank, and he gave the situation some thought.

The door to the house next door creaked open. "Quiet, Mish!" Pete said under his breath, and slowly stood up.

"Oh, hello Mrs. Tribble," he called out.

Mrs. Tribble peered over at him. "Oh there you

are," she said. "Well, thank goodness, I didn't wait for you! I got right out there with my broom and then I came in and called the dog pound. I'm not one who will stand for the neighborhood overrun with dogs, I'll tell you. It's been right nice on this block since that teacher's been gone. I don't mind telling you I for one don't miss that big black dog of hers!"

Pete glanced quickly down at his feet. Mishmash grinned wickedly, and his tail switched.

Mrs. Tribble looked up and down the street. "I guess they're hiding," she said, and she sounded sorry. "All of them, hiding. I told the dogcatcher he'd better hurry." She went in and slammed the door.

From down the street Pete heard the advancing sound of a motor. He put his hand on Mishmash's collar. "Come on Mish!" he said. "We'd better get out of here."

Mish ambled agreeably along as Pete hurried him up the steps and put his hand on the door. It was locked. Pete's heart began to beat louder. He tried the door again. The sound of the car turning the corner bore down on him. Pete looked at Mishmash.

The dog grinned back as if he were rather pleased with himself for keeping the house so well guarded.

"The key!" Pete said. "Mish! Where's the key!" But Mishmash only twitched his nose and grinned some more.

6

PETE HAD NO TIME for games. He grabbed Mishmash by the collar, dragged him off the porch and around the house. He led him under the fence and across the churchyard and through another neighbor's yard. It wasn't until he reached his own backyard that he remembered about the rummage sale going on next door.

Pete stood still.

Ladies were coming out of the Sparlings' house and talking loudly in the Sparlings' backyard. Stuff was hanging all over the place. On the cherry tree and the apple tree. Over the back fence and piled up on card tables. There were hats and shoes and umbrellas, toys, lamps, bedspreads, books and dishes. There was an old TV set, a clock radio, a lawn mower and Mrs. Sparling's old fur coat.

"Oh my!" Pete could hear someone say. And, "Did you ever!" and "Where did she ever find such a thing!" and the sort of things ladies say when they aren't really saying anything.

The curtain in the upstairs window of his own house flapped. Quickly Pete led Mishmash around to the back door. His mother was up in the bedroom. The way was clear.

Mishmash scrambled up onto Pete's bed. He tested it, seemingly, by slapping at the pillow with his paw. Then he turned all the way around and sat with his head resting on the middle of the bed and his back end on the pillow.

"Good old Mish!" Pete said fondly. He remembered the time when Mishmash had taken the whole bed for himself and left Pete to sleep on the rug on the floor. Pete grinned. Mish hadn't changed much, living with Miss Patch. Except that his grin looked even more like the teacher's.

Funny, he thought, how dogs grow to look like the people who own them. A cross dog usually belongs to an owner who looks angry. A sad faced dog always seems to belong to someone who seldom smiles. A person like Miss Patch would just naturally match up with a happy dog like Mishmash. There never was a teacher like Miss Patch, and — so far as Pete knew — there wasn't another dog like Mishmash, either. Mishmash and Miss Patch belonged together.

Pete patted Mishmash's sleek head. Mishmash opened his eyes, raised his eyelids a fraction and let them flutter closed again.

Softly Pete closed the bedroom door behind him, and went downstairs.

Mrs. Peters was standing before the little mirror in the entryway putting on her hat. Mr. Peters came down the stairway, too. "You going somewhere?" he asked Mrs. Peters.

"Next door. To the rummage sale." Mrs. Peters patted her hat and began to pull on her gloves.

"You putting on a hat to walk next door?" Pete asked.

His mother made a little face at him. "Of course! It's a party!"

"And she just saw that Mrs. Barnes walk in

wearing a hat with a big pink flower and a ribbon," suggested Mr. Peters.

Pete met his father's glance and they both
grinned. But his mother didn't see anything funny
in it at all.

"If you need me, I'll be right next door," she
said gaily, and opening the door, she went carefully down the walk in her best high heels.

There was a bang from upstairs in the bedroom.

"What's that?" said Mr. Peters, but he wasn't
too interested. He opened the refrigerator door
and stuck his head inside.

Pete raised his eyes but the rest of him froze
still. "I guess my book must have fallen off my
desk," he said offhandedly.

His father turned to look at him. "By itself?"

Pete shrugged. "I guess I must have left it too
near the edge — or something." He made himself
walk slowly out of the kitchen and up the stairway. He pretended not to notice his father gazing
after him. But as soon as he made the turn, he
dashed down to his room.

Mishmash was standing on the desk looking out the window over Mrs. Sparling's backyard. He turned to grin at Pete.

"Down! Mishmash," Pete ordered. "Down!" But Mishmash only moved over. Pete looked out too.

There was a very good view of the backyard. A brisk business was going on at the coffee and cake table, as far as Pete could see, but business elsewhere was lagging.

By sticking his head way out the window, Pete could see the hat booth. With a feeling of disappointment, he saw that Wanda was taking care of that. She was using the old apple tree as a hat bar. He could just make out the London bobby's hat stuck on a branch. The branch was almost hanging into Pete's yard. Pete calculated the distance between his side of the fence and the branch which held the hat.

"Keep your eye on it, Mishmash," he whispered. Then he went out of the room. He moved quietly down the stairs and outside. Keeping his head low, he ran from the house to the side of the fence, then moved slowly along the fence. Just below the hanging hat, he crouched low, breathing slowly, so that Wanda would not hear him.

Carefully he raised his hand, inch by inch. His fingers curved so that at the right moment he could flip the hat off the limb and drop down. Boy! Wouldn't old Wanda be surprised! He snickered and grabbed.

But his fingers only clutched at nothing, and he looked at the bare branch in surprise.

Wanda's head appeared over the fence. "That's not for sale!" she said. "That one's for display purposes only!"

Pete scowled at her. Then he walked back across the yard and into his house.

When he returned to his room, Mishmash lay stretched out on the bed. His chest was moving rapidly up and down as if he had been running, and his tongue hung down out of the side of his mouth. Resting on his ears was a hat — a lady's hat with a pink flower and a ribbon.

Pete looked out the window to the porch next door where some of the women had laid aside their scarves and hats — and he groaned.

At the sound Mishmash opened one eye. He looked down his nose at Pete, and then rolled his eye back under his eyelid.

The noise of the party next door floated upward. Mrs. Sparling was standing on a chair ringing a bell.

"Ladies! May I have your attention a moment, ladies! Has anybody seen Mrs. Barnes' hat?" she called. "She laid it down for a moment and someone — well, I'm afraid someone might have mistaken it for part of the rummage."

A titter ran through the ladies and Mrs. Barnes looked as if she was getting mad. "It was a brandnew hat!" she said loudly.

Pete turned back to the bed. He pulled Mishmash off. "Get it back down there, Mish!" he said crossly. "You hear me! You take that right back. Set it on the chair or something, or maybe on the porch. Only don't come back up here until you return it. You understand!"

Mishmash gave him a considering look, then he moved slowly across the room. Pete opened the door, checked the hallway and motioned Mish out. Mishmash went down the hallway with the hat on his head.

Pete ran back to the window. In a moment, he saw Mishmash down there on the driveway with the hat still on his head. Then Pete gasped.

For Mishmash was walking right down the front walk out to the sidewalk. He wasn't intending to return the hat at all!

Suddenly Mrs. Barnes came running out to the front. "My hat!" she shrieked. "That animal is wearing my hat!"

Pete leaned out the window. "Wait, Mish!" he hollered. "Wait!"

But Mish evidently had no intention of waiting. With a shake of his head, he flung off the hat, and ran.

7

PETE STOOD in Miss Patch's front yard and examined the house carefully. The window shade was halfway up again, the door was locked. Pete stood listening. He wondered if Mishmash could be hiding in there.

Pete walked around to the back and looked into the kitchen window. Everything was exactly the way Miss Patch had left it.

As he stepped off the back porch he saw a small mound of turned up earth at the side. It looked as if a hole had been dug and then filled up again. Pete couldn't remember seeing it before. His heart began to pound and he bent quickly and began digging at the soft earth with a stick. The stick struck something, and Pete pried the object up. He picked it up and shook the dirt off it. It was a can. He turned it around. An empty sauerkraut can!

Thoughtfully Pete looked at it. It had been opened with a can opener. Pete wondered how Mishmash had managed to open it so neatly. He held it a moment in his hand, then dropped it back into the hole and covered it up. He stood looking at the spot at which the can was buried. It proved something to him all right. It proved that Mishmash was the sauerkraut thief!

Looking around the yard, Pete wondered whether the whole yard was filled with buried sauerkraut cans. Miss Patch would be pretty mad when she went to plant her daffodil bulbs and found a can everywhere she dug a hole. Pete went back around to the front of the house again.

Putting his face into his new grimace, Pete stared hard at the dusty porch. The footprints there were all his own size. He dragged out the broom and halfheartedly swept. But he kept looking up and down the street and glancing to the corners of the house hoping to see Mishmash's grinning face. He didn't see anything. He hadn't seen anything of Mishmash for three days. Not since the day of Mrs. Sparling's rummage sale.

Glumly Pete picked up the welcome mat and banged it against the side of the porch to loosen the dirt. Mrs. Tribble opened the door of her house and came out to peer over the hedge.

"Oh, it's you!" she said.

Slowly Pete crossed the lawn.

"I haven't been hearing so many noises lately," she whispered, nodding as if she were responsible.

"Hardly any at all!" She shook her finger playfully. "I must be the only person in the world who has perfected a poltergeist eradicator," she said.

Pete's mouth fell open.

She leaned closer to him. "I set it out every night and I take it in every morning." Carefully she glanced around before drawing something out of her apron pocket.

In her hands was an old-fashioned alarm clock. It had a big white face and black hands. There was a little hammer and bell near the ring at the top. Pete looked at it closely. It was the one he had seen at Mrs. Sparling's rummage sale.

"But it doesn't tell the right time!" said Pete.

Mrs. Tribble gave him a respectful look. "You are very smart, boy. No it doesn't. But neither can the poltergeists. They're afraid of time, I've discovered. I've set this clock out every night and taken it in every morning for the last three days and there have been less and less of those funny noises next door, I can tell you, they're almost gone!" She leaned down to whisper, "It's the ticking!"

Pete opened his mouth and closed it again without saying anything. It wasn't the poltergeists who were gone; it was Mishmash.

Mrs. Tribble was examining her clock with appreciation. "I got it from a lady up the street who had it left over from her rummage sale," she said. "Imagine giving a rummage sale of your old stuff in your backyard. Some people do the craziest things, don't they?"

Pete looked at her, and then at the clock.

"Picked it up for just twenty-five cents," Mrs. Tribble said in a satisfied tone. "It's good as new except it doesn't tell good time." She turned it over and began to wind it. "Sometimes the biggest problems have the simplest solutions," she said. Then she put her alarm clock back into her apron pocket. And nodding once or twice she made her way back into her house.

Pete looked after her thoughtfully. Then he put away the lawn mower. As he was going out the gate, a station wagon stopped in front of Miss Patch's house. On its side it said: "We-take-good-care-of-your-dog Kennel." A man got out. He looked at the house and then at Pete.

"You live here?" he said.

Pete shook his head.

The man scratched his head. "You haven't seen a dog hanging around here, have you. A big black dog?"

"Not the last three days," Pete said, wishing he had.

"Crazy dog," muttered the man with a frown. "Give him everything a dog could want — a cement yard, plenty to eat, and lots of company — and what does he do? He runs away! Can you beat that? He opens the gate himself and walks right

out!" The man stared angrily at Pete. "I had to go
and put locks on everything — he wised all the
other dogs up, that's what he did!"

"Is that so?" said Pete, pretending to be surprised.

The man sighed and got back into his car. He
cranked down the window. "I've been looking
for him," he said. "Every two-three days I go out
to look for him." Suddenly his face turned red.
" 'A friendly dog,' she said!" He started the motor,
muttering to himself and went off.

Pete stood there looking after him. He wished the man would find Mishmash before Miss Patch arrived home. He certainly wished he would. Pete walked slowly down the street.

"I can't understand why Mishmash ran away from me like that," he told Wanda later that afternoon.

"I can," said Wanda. "It's because you yelled at him and hurt his feelings. People who live alone always get their feelings hurt easily," she observed.

"Of course, I'm not saying Mishmash is exactly alone," Wanda hinted, "but he probably feels lonesome. For Miss Patch."

Pete thought of Mishmash feeling lonely for Miss Patch. He scowled. "He's only been living alone for a little while," he said.

"My Uncle Harris was only home alone for three days once and he got so lonely he came over and slept at our house. He didn't like it though," Wanda added thoughtfully. "He thought we should let him choose the TV programs because he was a guest." She grinned wickedly. "My mother says anyone who sleeps more than two nights in our house is a member of the family — no matter who he thinks he is. My Uncle Harris put on his hat and walked out the front door and we haven't seen him since."

"Where did he go?" Pete asked, interested even though he didn't want to be.

Wanda shrugged. "We got a postcard once, but there was nothing on it. Just the picture."

"How do you know the postcard was from your Uncle Harris?"

Wanda grinned. "My Uncle Harris is the only one in the family who won't write on a postcard. He thinks the postman might read it."

Pete looked at her, feeling a little impatient. "We're talking about Mishmash," he reminded her. Suddenly he remembered how smart Mishmash was. "Probably he is already on his way back to Miss Patch's," he said brightly.

"Not if he left the window shade halfway up," Wanda pointed out.

Pete pressed his mouth into the upside-down half circle.

"Maybe the man from the We-take-good-care-of-your-dog Kennel will find him," he said hopefully.

Wanda snorted.

"Well, we could put an ad in the newspaper." Pete was thinking hard. "We could say — Lost. Black Dog."

"The town is full of black dogs," Wanda sniffed.

"Not like Mishmash. If we could word the ad to describe him . . ."

"My mother says there aren't any words to describe Mishmash—that's what my mother says!"

Pete held himself still a moment. "All right," he said then. "All right!" And he walked into his house and slammed the door.

Mrs. Peters was standing in the hallway sorting out the mail. "My goodness!" she said. "What's this?"

"What's what?" said Pete, but he didn't really care. He started up the stairs.

"A postcard!" she said and she sounded surprised.

Pete whirled around.

Mrs. Peters looked at it a moment and turned it over. "Well, for goodness sakes!" she said.

Pete felt his heart begin to beat loudly. Of course he knew that Mishmash couldn't possibly . . .

"Does it say anything?" he asked anxiously.

His mother glanced at him with an odd expression. "Of course it says something," she said. "It says:

"Dear Mrs. Peters: I have a feeling that I went off and left the back door unlocked. Will you please ask Pete to check it for me. It only locks on the inside so he'll have to open the door, reach in and turn the latch, and close the door firmly again. Miss Patch."

"Oh!" Pete said. "It's from Miss Patch." He couldn't account for the feeling of disappointment that engulfed him.

His mother looked at him closely. "You'd better take care of that right away."

"Sure," said Pete, and walked slowly up the stairs.

8

AT MISS PATCH'S HOUSE the next morning, Pete didn't bother to get out the lawn mower. He checked the back door. But it didn't surprise him any to find that it was locked. Mish must have left it that way. Then he walked around the house a couple of times. Once he called, "Here, Mishmash. Come here boy," softly under his breath. But he knew Mishmash wasn't there. Pete walked out the front gate and down the street.

A woman carrying a sackful of groceries came toward him.

"Did you see a black dog around here?" he asked.

She shook her head.

Pete went on. He looked up every street and into every yard. Once he thought he saw a large dark shape behind some shrubbery, but it was only a big cat.

He came to a small park. A sign said: NO DOGS ALLOWED. Hopefully Pete walked into the park but he didn't catch sight of Mishmash.

An old lady sat on a bench.

"You didn't see a black dog running around here, did you?" he asked.

She looked at him with a severe expression. "It's against the law to let a dog run around without a leash, young man. If you've lost your dog, you'd better find him quick before the Humane Society people do. They've been cruising around here all morning."

Pete raised his head. "Around here?"

She nodded briskly. "I saw their truck not two minutes ago sneaking around. They always sneak around," she said disapprovingly. "If you go through the park and around that building, you'll probably see it yourself."

Slowly Pete walked in the direction she had pointed. He went through the park and crossed the street. A lady held a little black poodle on a leash. The lady wore a ribbon on top of her head and a pink necklace around her throat. The dog wore a ribbon too and his collar was sprinkled with pearls. They both wore the same expression on their face, thought Pete, and he grinned.

Pete walked on. A woman stood at the curb beside her car, talking to a policeman. Pete stopped.

"This big black dog grinned at me," she said. "I tell you, he grinned at me!"

The policeman took off his hat and scratched his head. "Look, lady, there's no law I know of against grinning. Any person has a right to grin, when he wants to."

"But officer, that's what I'm trying to tell you. This wasn't a person. This was a dog!"

Pete's heart lifted. He pretended to be looking at the buns in the bakery window. Down the street, a horn honked. Pete looked up.

The lady got into her car still talking, and the officer winked at Pete. Up the street the horn kept right on honking. His grin changed to a look of puzzlement, and he turned and began to walk rapidly toward the sound.

Pete hurried too. A crowd had gathered in front of a drugstore. Parked at the curb, was a little red car. It was a neat little red sports car with the top down.

"What's going on here?" asked the policeman.

A man was waving his arms around talking excitedly. "Look, officer," he said. "I just stopped a moment, to run in to get a box of candy. I left my car out front with the motor running. Just for a minute, you understand."

The officer frowned.

"All I was going to do was pick up this box of candy," he said, waving a box tied in a red ribbon under the officer's nose. "So I go in and I pick up my box and I hear someone honking my horn. As if someone was saying hurry up, y'know. So I came running out and — well, you won't believe it — but here was this big black hound sitting in the back seat, comfortable-like, you know, with his foot stretched out pressing on my horn. Honestly officer, on my honor!"

The officer took his hat off again. He looked around. Some of the people were grinning. "Did

anybody see any dog honking this guy's horn?" he asked the crowd.

No one said anything.

"Now look here, officer," the man said. "It just happens no one was around!"

The officer pulled out his notebook. "You say a dog was sitting in your car honking for you?"

Someone in the crowd laughed.

The man nodded. There was a worried look on his face.

"Well, whose dog was it?" the officer asked. He looked around.

Pete stepped back. He tried to hide his smile. It was Mishmash all right. Mishmash was close by!

"Well, where is this so-called dog now?" the officer asked.

No one answered. Pete started to walk away. But he walked slowly and casually until he reached the corner, and then he ran. It was Mishmash all right! He knew it was Mishmash. He must have been trying to get a ride with the man, just as he was trying to get a ride with the woman. Pete remembered how Mishmash loved to ride. Pete stood still and looked around. "Mishmash!" he called under his breath.

On the next block stood a small truck with its back door open. Pete began to walk faster. The driver came out of the store, slammed the back door shut without looking inside and got into the front seat. Pete broke into a run. He reached the car just as it pulled away. On its side was a name — COUNTY HUMANE SOCIETY.

"Mishmash!" shouted Pete.

A familiar black face appeared at the wire mesh-covered window on the back of the truck. The truck swerved a little and then picked up speed.

Mish grinned, his tongue hanging at the side of his mouth, his ears gently lifting in the breeze.

9

Pete walked into the building marked Humane Society. "I'm looking for a dog," he said to the man at the desk.

The man smiled. "Well, we've got lots of dogs here. When did you lose him?"

Pete frowned. "I didn't exactly lose him," he said.

"A runaway," said the man. "We got plenty of those too." He pulled a pad of paper before him. "What's his license number?"

"Well, I'm not sure —"

The man looked at him sternly. "You have to have a license for a dog you own in this city," he said.

"Well, I don't exactly own him —" Pete said and he knew he had said the wrong thing.

The man pushed the blank form away. "Look, kid," he said kindly. "If you want a dog, you have to pay a dollar, and you can go in and pick one out. But you can't get any kind of a dog for nothing, do you understand?"

Pete nodded. He said quickly. "You mean if I pay a dollar, I can go in there and pick out any dog I want?"

"That's right, sonny. You can have your pick of the strays."

Eagerly, Pete nodded. He followed the man through a back door, down a narrow hallway and through another door. As soon as it was opened, the noise surrounded them. The place was divided into wire rooms. Heavy mesh separated one space from another. Each held dogs. And all of the dogs were barking.

"You can have most anyone you take a fancy to," the man said.

A loud howl came from the other end of the room. It was Mishmash. Pete made himself walk slowly down the aisle way. He looked into each

cage, taking time to inspect a number of different dogs. He walked right past Mishmash's cage the first time, pretending he had never seen the grinning black dog before.

"Say," said the man. "Does that dog know you?"

"Which dog?" said Pete, looking the other way on purpose.

"The big black one. Acts as if he knows you."

Pete turned slowly and pretended to inspect Mishmash. "Hmmm," he said. "That's so. I guess maybe he likes me. I guess that's the one I want," he said. "I'll take him."

This is easy, he thought, trying not to smile. Once he got him home, he wouldn't let him get away again.

The man shook his head. "Sorry, kid. That one just came in this morning. We have to keep our pickups three days. If no one claims them in three days, then we get rid of them, anyway we can."

"I guess maybe I'll wait then," said Pete. But he couldn't seem to see very well as he followed the man back down the long room, and all he could hear was Mishmash howling pitifully behind him.

As Mr. Peters read the newspaper the next morning, he chuckled softly.

Mrs. Peters filled Pete's milk glass and looked at her husband.

"Seems there was a regular jailbreak down at the Humane Society last night," Mr. Peters said.

Pete put down his glass of milk.

Mr. Peters looked at the newspaper again and smiled. "Some dog they picked up yesterday organized all the hounds and set them to howling at midnight."

"That's impossible!" said Mrs. Peters.

"What happened?" Pete asked.

"It made such a racket that the police came out. But when they unlocked the door to see what it was all about, the dogs streaked out. It says here the dogcatcher was up all night trying to round them up."

Pete held his breath. "Did they get them all?"

"They're still looking for one or two," his father said, turning the page. "They can't find the ringleader."

Pete smiled. He drank his milk, and he smiled some more.

"Does it say anything about the sauerkraut thief?" Mrs. Peters asked a little anxiously.

Mr. Peters looked through the newspaper. "Here's something," he said. "A salesman found a couple of cans lying in his alley when he went to burn up some cartons. The police figured they might have fallen off a moving vehicle some days ago."

"Well, I guess I'd better get to my job," Pete said casually. He wondered whether a dog could be called a moving vehicle. But he was careful not to ask. Pretending not to notice his mother's eyes on him, he stuck a ball into his back pocket, pressed his face into the expression he liked best, and opened the door.

Mrs. Peters sighed and Pete closed the door carefully behind him.

He walked down the street, grinning. Wanda slammed the door of her house and came running out. She caught up with him.

"News report," Pete said out of the side of his mouth. "Guess who checked out of the dog pound last night."

Wanda sniffed. "If he's smart he'll lie low. My mother says they've even got police cars cruising for him."

"She doesn't have to worry," Pete said airily. "Not if it's Mishmash."

Wanda snorted. "You're right there!" she said. "She doesn't have to. But you do. Personally, if I were you, I'd wash my hands of the whole affair."

Pete looked at his hands. His baseball was still held in one. Pete began tossing his ball into the air and catching it again. Walking along, they reached Jules Ivar's house. Pete paid no attention to the peculiar sound Wanda made through her teeth. Something like a hiss.

Mrs. Ivar came out of her house. She opened the mailbox and took out a letter.

"You hear anything from Jules?" Pete asked eagerly.

She looked up and smiled. "Oh my yes. He's very good about writing." She opened the mailbox and took out a letter.

"I hardly knew he was even gone," Wanda said, looking steadily at Pete.

"He's won more points than anyone in the camp so far!" said Mrs. Ivar proudly. "I expect he'll be getting the fastest swimming medal."

"Wow!" said Pete.

"I'm sure that's very nice," said Wanda in the polite way ladies talk when they aren't much interested.

"I have to laugh when I think of how I had to talk myself blue in the face to get him to agree to go to camp this year." Mrs. Ivar smiled happily. "The fastest swimmer!" she said proudly. "Imagine that!"

Pete nodded. It wasn't hard for him to imagine that at all. "I guess he can be the best at anything he wants to," Pete said in fond admiration.

"Well, I wouldn't be a bit surprised." Mrs. Ivar turned the letter over. She glanced at the envelope and looked at it again closely. "That's funny," she said. "It's postmarked right here in this neighborhood."

Wanda patted her mouth to cover a yawn. "When I went to camp, sometimes the counselor would bring the whole batch of mail into town to be mailed," she suggested politely.

Mrs. Ivar smiled. "That must be it," she said and looking into the mailbox again, pulled out a postcard. She read it aloud.

"Dear Mrs. Ivar,

We are so sorry to hear that your son will not be able to attend camp this session, and hope that he will be back with us soon again.

Yours very truly,

John Bittleford, Camp Director."

She laughed. "Must be some mistake," she said. I'll have to write them and tell them so." She turned and smiled at Pete and Wanda, and went back into the house.

Pete thought of Mishmash leading the whole dog pound out in the middle of the night. Pete couldn't help it. He laughed out loud.

"What's so funny?" said Wanda, squinting at him as if she didn't like what she saw.

"Mishmash," Pete said. "Good old Mishmash."

Thoughtfully Wanda gazed at him. "Good old Mishmash," she said dryly.

Pete pressed his face into Jules upside-down inquiring smile.

"Now — all you've got to do is find him," Wanda said. "You've got to find him pretty soon. Because pretty soon is when Miss Patch will be home!" And she walked on without him.

10

ANOTHER FEW DAYS went by. Each day Pete studied Miss Patch's house carefully. Each day he scouted the neighborhood. No Mishmash.

"He's hiding," he told Wanda. "He's just hiding out somewhere." But secretly he worried. Mish wasn't the kind of dog who could hide out by himself very long. Sooner or later he'd want to do what people were doing.

Thoughtfully Pete walked up and down in front of the neighborhood movie theater. He kept an eye on the people coming out but there was no sign of Mishmash. Then he went down to the supermarket. But though he spent a whole afternoon, he didn't see Mishmash there either.

Once he thought he saw the dog. An old man with a shopping bag on his arm came walking stiffly along and behind him tagged a black dog.

"Mishmash," shouted Pete.

The dog stopped, but the old man turned on Pete with a snarl. "You get out of here, boy! You understand!" he said meanly. "This dog knows where he belongs."

For a moment the dog looked as if he were going to grin, but it came out a kind of snarl too, and he followed after his master who had him well secured with a brand-new rope around his sleek black neck.

Pete looked after them with a strange feeling. The dog was walking stiff-legged too, just like his master, and on his face was the same grumpy expression. Yet Pete stood still and looked after them. He looked after them for a long time.

A few days later, Wanda came hurrying over after dinner. "I saw Mishmash!" she said in a loud whisper."

Pete felt his heart jump. "Where?"

"At least I think it was Mishmash," Wanda said, and Pete thought he knew what she was going to say.

"You saw him with an old man," he said wearily. "And he snarled."

Wanda shook her head. "It was a young man. He was standing on the corner whistling at the girls. And Mishmash — at least this dog I thought was Mishmash — was helping him."

"You mean Mishmash was whistling?"

"Well, it looked as if he was whistling. But I couldn't be sure. Anyway he was grinning. He was grinning just the way this fellow was. Then this fellow went inside the store and they wouldn't let this dog in, and he got mad and walked off with his nose in the air."

It sounded like Mishmash. It certainly sounded like him. Pete looked at Wanda fondly.

"It was on Cherry Avenue," Wanda said. "I would have followed him, but my dentist's office is right upstairs over the drugstore and he opened his window and leaned out and yelled at me. I guess I was a little late for my appointment," she said reflectively.

Pete made his way to Cherry Avenue. He stood on the corner awhile and looked for a young man who whistled at girls but the only person who crossed the street was a lady in slacks and a kid sucking a Popsicle.

"Did you see a fellow around here with a big black dog?" Pete asked the kid. "A great big dog."

The kid took his popsicle out of his mouth and began to cry. His mother looked back.

"All I did was ask him if he saw a dog," Pete said, hurriedly.

The woman frowned. "He's afraid of dogs," she said. She came back, took the kid's hand, stuck the Popsicle back into his open mouth and pulled him into a store.

Glumly Pete looked after them. A man came out of the shoe shop.

"Did I hear you asking about Mike Boyle?"

"Who?" said Pete.

"Mike. The kid who used to hang around here."

"I guess so," said Pete.

"He isn't here anymore," said the man. "Got a job I understand. In Alaska." He turned to go back into the store.

"But the dog!" Pete said.

"You looking for a dog?" The man said, as if this was the first he'd heard of it.

Eagerly Pete nodded.

"Why don't you try the Humane Society," he suggested. "That place must be full of dogs." And he went back into his store.

Pete walked on down the street.

"Here, Mish," he called experimentally, once or twice. But his voice didn't hold much hope. In a few days Miss Patch was due home. And he'd have to tell her how he had helped Mishmash hide out, and how he had lost him.

"Here Mish!" Pete called again, louder, as he walked along. "Where are you, Mish?"

A man standing out on the sidewalk sprinkling his rosebushes looked at him oddly. Pete stopped.

"You haven't seen a black dog around here lately, have you?" he asked.

The man turned the nozzle of his sprinkler to a fine spray. "You mean Mrs. Elderberry's dog?" he asked.

"I guess not," Pete said.

"She lives over in the old gray house." He jerked his head to one of the houses across the street. Pete didn't even bother to look at it.

"Oh, you won't catch sight of her," the man said as if Pete had been staring at the place. "Hardly anybody ever sees her. Nobody even knew she had a dog until just the other day."

"Is that so?" said Pete politely. He squatted down to rest a little.

The man looked over his shoulder as if to make sure no one was listening. "She doesn't seem to trust people," he said lowering his voice. "Not even the mailman. Makes him leave the circulars on the first step on the porch. Won't even open the door to the grocery boy. He leaves the groceries in the garage. Although how she stays alive, he doesn't know. He delivers mostly birdseed and tea bags. Eats like a bird, my wife says." Then he laughed. "The bird seed is for her canary."

Pete looked curiously across the street.

The man's voice dropped to a whisper. "Afraid of her own shadow, that woman is. She gets up half a dozen times a night, my wife says, to look under the bed. In case there might be burglars or something, y'know." He chuckled. "The only time she ever comes out is to go to funerals. That's her recreation, you might say. My wife says she feels right comfortable crying. Some people do, you know." He looked at Pete with a twinkle.

102

Pete sighed.

The man turned the nozzle full force again.

"As I was saying, I noticed a black dog sitting on her porch only yesterday."

Pete raised his head.

"But it's her dog all right. He hides his head under the newspaper every time someone walks by. Afraid of people, just like she is."

The man turned the water down again and looked out across the street. "It's kind of funny, when you think of it, I guess. She's not afraid of animals. Just people."

"Thanks," said Pete. But he wasn't quite sure what for.

"Not Mishmash," he said to Wanda when he got back home. And he couldn't help sighing. Then he pressed his face into a knowing grimace. "But he's somewhere," he said. "He's got to be somewhere."

"Sometimes people disappear," said Wanda solemnly. "Sometimes they just disappear off the face of the earth. They're never seen or heard of again. Pffffft! Just like that." She gave him a wary look. "Sort of like the sauerkraut thief," she suggested.

Pete gave his best imitation of Jules Ivar's derisive laugh. But somehow it came out sounding more like a sob. Quickly he pressed his face into a frown.

Wanda pulled something out from under the porch. She stuck it into his hands. "Here's what you wanted," she said. "I've been meaning to give it to you. I thought it might make you feel better. Losing Mishmash, and Miss Patch coming home soon, I mean."

Pete pressed his mouth down harder. In his hands Wanda had placed a hat — the English bobby's hat. "Thanks," he muttered. But it didn't make him feel any better. Somehow, Wanda being nice to him made him feel even worse.

He placed the hat on his head and went quickly into his house.

11

"Miss PATCH is home!" Mrs. Peters said, and looked at him in a worried way.

Pete closed the door slowly behind him.

"She just telephoned," his mother said. "She said she thinks someone has been using her house as a hideout."

Pete stood very still.

"You don't suppose someone could have been living in there all the while she was gone, do you?" Mrs. Peters said.

"I guess maybe someone could," Pete said, but he didn't look at his mother. He wondered if Miss Patch knew it was Mishmash.

"She said there was even some ice cream in the refrigerator. Pistachio."

"Pistachio!" Pete couldn't help shouting. His

mother gave him a funny look. It was odd, he thought, that Mishmash should choose pistachio.

Mrs. Peters sighed. "Well, I, for one, am glad she's home."

Pete walked out of the house over to Wanda's. He sat heavily down on her porch step.

"News report," he said grimly. "Miss Patch is home. She thinks someone has been using her house as a hideout." He laughed hollowly. Then unaccountably his face twisted up. The thought of Miss Patch finding out how he had helped Mishmash and then gone and lost him gave him a real pain.

"Maybe Miss Patch won't find out," Wanda said helpfully. "Maybe she'll think Mishmash ran away from the kennel and just never came back."

"I'll have to tell her," said Pete.

"You'll what!" shrieked Wanda. She covered her mouth with her hand. They both waited breathlessly to make sure no one in the Sparling kitchen had heard them.

"Don't be silly!" Wanda said then. "Why would you have to tell her, for heaven's sake?"

Pete only looked at her. "I just have to, that's all."

"But if you didn't tell her, she wouldn't know. And if she didn't know she wouldn't blame you."

"I'll have to tell her," Pete said.

Wanda fell silent. "All right," she said suddenly. "We'll both tell her. We'll both go right up to her and explain how it happened. If she's going to blame you, she'll have to blame me too. You and me equally." Wanda's eyes gleamed in the dark.

Pete stood up. "You stay out of this, Wanda Sparling!" he shouted.

The back door flew open. "Wanda, you come in here this moment," Wanda's mother said.

Wanda made a face at Pete, and went in.

His father gazed at him balefully across the breakfast table the next morning.

"Is there something I should know about?" Mr. Peters hinted.

Pete carefully picked out the sliced peaches which had been laid over his cereal, and put them at the side of his plate. He shrugged.

His mother looked at his father, delicately shaking her head. "Suppose we let Pete tell us — whatever he wants to tell us, that is," she said.

"There's nothing to tell," said Pete. "Nothing I want to tell, that is," he amended quickly.

This time Mr. and Mrs. Peters both looked at him. But Pete pretended not to notice. His father picked up the newspaper, and turned the pages slowly.

"Anything new?" his mother asked in the bright way she talked when she was pretending she wasn't worried about anything.

"Hmmmm," said his father, and looked up and down the columns. "Here's something," he said suddenly. "They think they've caught that sauerkraut thief."

Pete choked on a mouthful of cereal, and had to push back his chair and wipe his collar with his napkin. "Where did they find him?" he asked when he could speak again.

Mr. Peters chuckled. "On a street corner downtown. He had set up an apple box and was selling sauerkraut two for the price of one."

"Selling!" shouted Pete. He had never thought that Mishmash would try to *sell* things.

His father went on reading from the newspaper.

"He was also caught with an unlicensed station wagon, three stolen bicycles, a wristwatch and — " Mr. Peters stopped to chuckle — "a Diner's Card. But he won't admit to anything."

Pete sat back in his chair. Not Mishmash.

"Imagine!" said Mrs. Peters, and smiled a little. "I guess he'll have a hard time getting anyone to believe him."

"Could be he didn't steal them," Pete said offhandedly, and then he ate the rest of his cereal without looking up.

Finishing his breakfast he went outside. He even pretended to whistle a little as he wheeled his bicycle out of the garage.

"I won't be long," he called dutifully to his mother. He pedaled slowly up the walk. Wanda came out of her house, ran down to the sidewalk and trotted beside him.

Pete scowled at her.

"I just thought I'd go along," she said. "Just to say hello to Miss Patch. That's all I'll say, just hello," she added hurriedly.

Pete nodded. He jumped off his bike and walked it along. He wished suddenly he hadn't brought his bike. He wasn't in a hurry to get to Miss Patch's anyway.

"Jules is home," said Wanda. "He came home yesterday. But he can't come out. His mother is

mad at him about something." Reflectively she looked back at his house. "Maybe he didn't win the fastest swimming medal after all."

Pete snorted. "Why would his mother be mad at him for *that!*"

"Funny," said Wanda. "Jules having to be first at everything."

"He doesn't have to," Pete said. "It's just that he wants to."

"That's what I mean," said Wanda.

They walked on together silently.

They reached the gas station. "Hey now!" called the service man. "The teacher's home!"

"I know," said Pete. Wanda nodded.

In front of the church, next door to Miss Patch's house, Pete stopped a moment to adjust the slant of his handlebar. He took a long time doing it, and he pretended that the odd beating in his chest had something to do with the effort he was putting forth.

The church door opened. "Nice morning!" called the Reverend Mr. Mulby.

Wanda waved her hand. Pete tried to smile, but

his face seemed stiff. He pushed the bike on, and leaned it carefully outside Miss Patch's gate. Wanda opened the gate.

"Well, come on," she said.

They walked up to the door together. The windows of Miss Patch's house were open, and the front door was ajar. Pete raised his hand to knock lightly at the door. Wanda pressed the bell.

The door opened wide. Miss Patch stood there. She wore an old school skirt and a blouse with a patched pocket.

"Come in!" she shouted when she saw who it was. For a moment, her teeth stuck out in her old friendly smile.

Pete didn't move to go in. His shoulders hunched forward. "I have to tell you about Mishmash!" he blurted.

Miss Patch nodded. "He was waiting for me," Miss Patch said. "He was sitting on the porch waiting for me when I arrived." And she reached behind her for a cleansing tissue, wiped her eyes and blew her nose.

12

Slowly Pete straightened up.

"You mean he's right here!" Wanda said.

"He's been staying here while you were gone," Pete said. "Most of the time."

"Oh!" said Miss Patch. "Well, that explains that!" Then a puzzled look came over her face. "Everything was dusted and straightened when I came home."

Pete twisted his lips into Jules Ivar's knowing smile. "Good old Mish," he said fondly, talking out of the side of his mouth.

The little wrinkle on Miss Patch's brow deepened. But she was not looking at Pete.

"He missed you," Pete said. "That's why he ran away from the kennel — and did other things," he finished with a warning glance at Wanda.

"Maybe that's why he's sick," said Miss Patch.

"Sick!" Pete and Wanda looked at each other. Miss Patch nodded and led them into the living room.

Mishmash lay on Miss Patch's leather chair. His big face rested on his paws. As they came near him, he opened his eyes, gave a great sigh and closed them again.

"That's all he does is sigh," said Miss Patch. "He lies there and rolls his eyes and sighs."

The dog opened his eyes, closed them again and — just as Miss Patch had said — sighed.

"He doesn't sleep well either. He was up every half hour or so last night. He'd get up and stick his head under the bed. I can't imagine what's the matter with him."

"Maybe it was the pistachio ice cream," Wanda said helpfully.

"He hardly eats at all!" said Miss Patch doubtfully. "He just nibbles. Sort of dainty bites, you know, as if he's afraid to swallow. It's funny," she said, "his throat seems to be all right."

"Could be his stomach," said Wanda. "We had

an uncle once who couldn't eat a thing. They said it was his stomach."

"What happened to him?" Pete asked.

Wanda shrugged. "He stopped coming to our house for Sunday dinner so I don't know."

"It's not his stomach," Miss Patch said. "I took him to the dog hospital first thing this morning, and they couldn't find a thing wrong with his stomach. To tell you the truth, the doctor wasn't sure what was wrong with him." Miss Patch's voice grew a little quavery. "They said I'd better bring him back and leave him — if he doesn't show any improvement."

"He's not going to like the hospital," Pete said. "Not if it's anything like the dog pound." And he made his words into a warning with Jules' twisted grimace.

Miss Patch regarded Pete for an instant with her head on one side. Pete pretended to be looking hard at Mishmash. He reached out and patted him gently. Mishmash raised his head, looked sorrowful and sighed. For a moment, it seemed to Pete as if Mishmash had enjoyed that sigh.

"Do they think he's really sick?" said Wanda.
Miss Patch nodded. "That's what they said.
He's not himself, is the way they put it." She gave
a wry little smile. Her smile stretched a bit and
broke down suddenly. "If a dog is suffering, and
they don't know what's wrong with him, they
think it's best to put him to sleep — for good."

"You mean he won't get well!" Wanda shrieked.

Miss Patch looked at Mishmash and seemed to be having trouble seeing. She blinked her eyes.

Mishmash barely lifted his head and sighed again, pitifully. He didn't sound like Mishmash, thought Pete. He sounded more like a little old lady.

A strange feeling began to crawl up the back of Pete's neck. For no reason at all he thought of Mrs. Elderberry who ate like a bird, looked under her bed at night and sighed all the time.

"I guess there's nothing to do but take him back to the hospital," Miss Patch said unhappily.

"Wait!" cried Pete.

Miss Patch jumped.

"He's not sick," Pete said slowly. "I don't think he's sick at all." He stared hard at Mishmash.

"Not sick?" said Miss Patch. She looked at Pete with surprise.

"I think he's just mixed up," Pete said hesitantly. And suddenly he was sure of it.

He began to tell Miss Patch how Mishmash had

been housekeeping for himself, and then how he had begun visiting around, staying with different people — until it was time for her to come home. Each time, the way dogs do, he took after the person he stayed with. When he was with the cross old man, he learned to snarl. When he was with the boy, he tried to whistle, and when he was with the lady who liked funerals he began to sigh.

Mishmash sighed again.

"Like that!" Pete said. "Just like that!"

"But that's almost unbelievable!" Miss Patch said.

Wanda nodded. "That's what my mother says. She says Mishmash is the most unbelievable dog she ever saw."

They all looked at Mishmash. He only rolled his sad eyes in his sad face. His dog mouth drifted downward. His tail lay limply against the cushion.

"Now look here, Mish," Pete said sternly. "A person's got to act like himself. That's what makes a person a person. And just because you're a dog is no excuse. Even a dog has to be himself. And no one else. You've got to be you! D'you hear me!"

Pete looked hard at the dog. He pressed his mouth down firmly at the corners so his chin felt hard and flat. Accidentally he caught sight of himself in Miss Patch's window glass. For a moment he was startled. It wasn't his face he glimpsed — it was Jules Ivar's!

Pete felt his neck grow warm. He stood a moment staring at the face in the glass. Then he slowly removed the English bobby's hat. He yanked the baseball out of his back pocket, and he smoothed the twists out of his mouth.

Mishmash raised his head, gravely watching him. The doorbell buzzed. Mishmash let his head sink down again. With a worried glance over her shoulder, Miss Patch went to open the door.

"Excuse me," said a high familiar voice.

Pete and Wanda looked at each other.

"My name is Jules. Jules Ivar."

"He lives down the street from us," Pete spoke up in explanation. "He's going to be in our room at school."

Miss Patch smiled. "Come in, Jules," she said.

Jules stumbled a little as he came in. His hair hung down as usual over his forehead. But he wasn't wearing his English bobby's hat. He looked as if he had forgotten all about wearing his hat.

"Hi Jules," Pete said.

Wanda didn't say anything.

"Hi," said Jules, but he was looking anxiously at Miss Patch with his face twisted up.

"My mother said I had to come and apologize," he said.

Miss Patch's mouth fell open.

"For staying in your house when I was supposed to be at camp."

Miss Patch gave a little gasp.

"I didn't hurt anything," Jules said hurriedly. "I brought my own food — except I didn't bring enough for *two*. So I had to borrow some."

"You stayed here!" said Miss Patch. She sounded as if she didn't believe it.

"You left the back door open," Jules said.

"You mean you didn't go to camp?" Pete said.

He was remembering the letters postmarked at the neighborhood post office.

"I sent a letter instead. Only I didn't figure they'd bother to acknowledge it."

"You didn't really win the swimming medal!" Wanda said.

Jules' face twisted up. "I never could swim very well," he said as if this explained everything. "My feet always sink."

"Oh," said Wanda as if she understood exactly what he meant.

"I figured if I hid out here, no one would know. But I didn't figure on him — " Jules jerked his head in the direction of Mishmash.

Pete didn't want to believe it. "If you were here with Mishmash, why didn't he come back here after he ran away with Mrs. Barnes' hat?"

"I guess he was mad at me. Because I kept the door locked and he couldn't open it when he wanted to. He wanted to bring all his friends into the house to play with him!" Jules looked accusingly at Mishmash.

121

Mishmash sighed.

"He went and dumped a whole basketful of someone's wet wash out on the laundromat floor. He was no help! He was no help at all."

It was Jules, not Mishmash, who turned the lights off and on, thought Pete. It was Jules who pulled up the window shade which Mishmash must have yanked down accidentally. It was Jules who ran the vacuum cleaner and dusted and locked and unlocked the door. It must have been Jules all the time. Pete felt disappointed.

He guessed Mishmash hadn't been housekeeping by himself after all. But he might have! Pete thought suddenly. Maybe he could have — if it hadn't been for Jules. Pete regarded Jules balefully.

"He eats an awful lot!" Jules said. He ate everything in sight — except some sauerkraut. It was lucky for me he didn't like sauerkraut," he added thoughtfully.

"The sauerkraut thief!" Wanda said triumphantly.

Miss Patch looked from one to the other in bewilderment.

"Not me!" Jules said quickly. "I found a whole caseful dumped in the alley. It fell off an old station wagon." His grimace was a smile. "Personally, I like sauerkraut very much."

"And pistachio," Miss Patch said and grinned.

"I buried the sauerkraut cans," Jules said anxiously. "It was the only garbage Mishmash wouldn't dig up."

"So you thought you'd hide out here instead of going to camp," Miss Patch said, looking at Jules carefully.

Wanda said, "It's because he thinks he's got to be best at everything."

Miss Patch nodded as if it sounded very reasonable to her. "Well, to my mind you can't be better than yourself. That's what I always say. And that's best enough for me!"

Jules looked at Miss Patch. He was smiling, Pete noticed, with both corners of his mouth turning evenly up.

Uncomfortably, Pete thought about himself trying to be like Jules. Then he thought of Mishmash acting like Mrs. Elderberry. He frowned — his old comfortable frown, and looked hard at the dog.

"Now as I was saying . . ." Pete said.

Miss Patch stuck her teeth out into a smile. Wanda giggled.

And Mishmash stood up and grinned.